The Zebra Said Shhh

M.R. Nelson   Tamia Sheldon

xist Publishing

It was bedtime at the zoo, but it was NOT quiet.
The animals were not sleeping.
They were all talking.

Up in his paddock, the zebra was
very, very tired,
but he could not go to sleep
because of the noise.

So the zebra said,
"Shhh, it's time to go to sleep."

But the monkeys did not
want to go to sleep.

They said, "ooo, ooo, ooo"
and swung around the trees.

The zebra said,
"Shhh, it's time to go to sleep."

The lion did not want
to go to sleep.

He said, "raaar"
and prowled around his den.

The zebra said,
"Shhh, it's time to go to sleep."

The parrot did not want
to go to sleep.

She said, "squawk, squawk"
and flew around
amongst the leaves.

The zebra said,
"Shhh, it's time to go to sleep."

The turtles did not want
to go to sleep.

They said, "snap, snap"
and lumbered around the yard
by their pond.

The zebra said,
"Shhh, it's time to go to sleep."

The seals did not want
to go to sleep.

They said, "ar, ar"
and splashed around
in their pool.

The zebra said,
"Shhh, it's time to go to sleep."

The giraffe did not want
to go to sleep.

She said, "munch, munch"
and chewed on the
leaves from her tree.

The zebra said,
"Shhh, it's time to go to sleep."

The hippopotamus did not want
to go to sleep.

He said, "snort, snort"
and rolled around
in the mud by his pond.

The zebra said,
"Shhh, it's time to go to sleep."

The rhinoceros did not want
to go to sleep.

She went, "stamp, stamp"
and stirred up the dust in
her field.

The zebra said,
"Shhh, it's time to go to sleep."

The polar bear did not want
to go to sleep.

He said, "grrrrr"
and stalked around the ice.

The zebra said,
"Shhh, it's time to go to sleep."

Suddenly, it got very quiet at the zoo.
None of the animals were talking anymore.
They were all asleep!

The monkeys were asleep
in their trees.

The lion was asleep in his den.

The parrot was asleep in her nest amongst the trees.

The turtles were asleep
by their pond.

The seals were asleep
by their pool.

The giraffe was asleep
by her tree.

The hippopotamus was asleep
in the mud.

The rhinoceros was asleep
in her field.

The polar bear was asleep
on the ice.

And up in his paddock,
the zebra said, "Shhh,"
and he closed his eyes
and went to sleep.

About the Author

M.R. Nelson discovered a love for telling stories when her oldest child began to demand them at times when reading someone else's stories out of a book was not possible. *The Zebra Said Shh* is her first published story, and is the story she tells most often, telling it almost every night at bedtime.

She lives in San Diego with her husband and two children.

About the Illustrator

Tamia Sheldon is a freelance illustrator and designer working outside of Seattle, WA.

She loves making up stories for her funny kid and spends all her free time drawing, reading and taking pictures. With a B.A. in Design and Culture Studies she is intent on creating work that has a positive impact on the world.

Don't Miss these Books from Xist Publishing

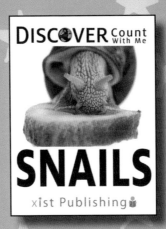

Made in the USA
Columbia, SC
07 November 2017